Lil' Red Pepper has a little red shop
in a place called Cherry Grove.
Lil' Red Pepper is very happy to live in such a great place.
Lil' Red Pepper is a very busy truck.
No time for shilly-shally in Cherry Grove.

PEPPER POWER!

In loving memory of Herm — B.W.

For AZ — L.M.

Special thanks to Kestrel Hendrickson
for artwork assistance.

ISBN 13: 978-1-59298-661-3
Library of Congress Catalog Number: 2018908333
Printed in the United States of America
First Printing: 2018
22 21 20 19 18   5 4 3 2 1

Edited by Lily Coyle

Beaver's Pond Press
7108 Ohms Lane
Edina, MN 55439–2129
(952) 829-8818
www.BeaversPondPress.com
To order, call (800)-901-3480.
Reseller discounts available.

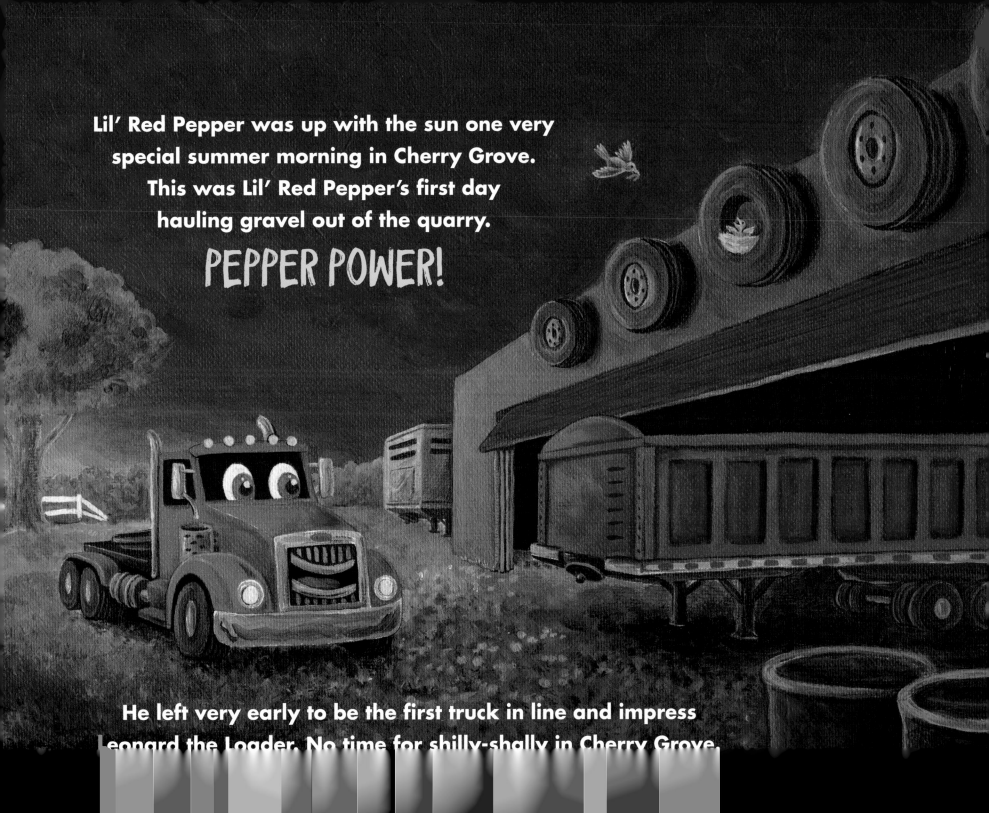

Lil' Red Pepper was up with the sun one very special summer morning in Cherry Grove. This was Lil' Red Pepper's first day hauling gravel out of the quarry.

PEPPER POWER!

He left very early to be the first truck in line and impress Leonard the Loader. No time for shilly-shally in Cherry Grove.

All the way to work Lil' Red Pepper was very excited but also nervous with first-day worries.
What if I make a mistake? Leonard the Loader might not want me back!
What if I run into Tough Troy? Tough Troy would squash me flat and
chew me up for scrap if he caught me in the wrong part of the quarry!

What if I get lost in the quarry? Trucks have gotten lost in the quarry
and never been seen or heard from since.
Lil' Red Pepper came to his senses. Stop worrying! There's no way I could get lost.
Jersey Jay gave me clear directions.

The sun rose higher and higher, but no other trucks came.

Lil' Red Pepper started to worry again.
Where's Leonard the Loader?
And where's everybody else? Surely other trucks
will be hauling out of the quarry today!

Lil' Red Pepper hustled over to the opposite end of the quarry.

Sure enough,
a line of trucks was
already waiting to load.
How did I make such a bad
mistake before the day even started?
Now I'll be at the back
of the line and
Leonard the Loader
will think
I'm lazy.

Lil' Red Pepper
nervously hurried down the winding haul
road toward the gravel pile. He was so upset
he missed a sharp turn and drove off the
road and got stuck. OH NO! Now what?

"You can't haul gravel when you're stuck in the sand, rookie!" hollered Jersey Jay.
"Quit your shilly-shallying and get to work!"
"Who taught you how to drive, kid?" Sassy Sal snorted, "Go back to school!"
Blue Barry yelled, "Why did Leonard the Loader hire a truck like you?"

Other trucks chimed in but all Lil' Red Pepper heard were mumbles and bumbles.

How did this morning go so wrong when it started off so well?

The other trucks laughed while Lil' Red Pepper spun his wheels.

I can't get out of this slippery sand and pretty soon I'm going to break down!

"PIPE DOWN!"

bellowed a voice from the top of the hill. It was the loudest and deepest voice Lil' Red Pepper had ever heard and it shook the quarry to a standstill.

It was Tough Troy,
the biggest tractor
in Cherry Grove!
Lil' Red Pepper was
so scared he
leaked oil.

Tough Troy rumbled
right up to Lil' Red Pepper,
blowing smoke and letting the dust fly.

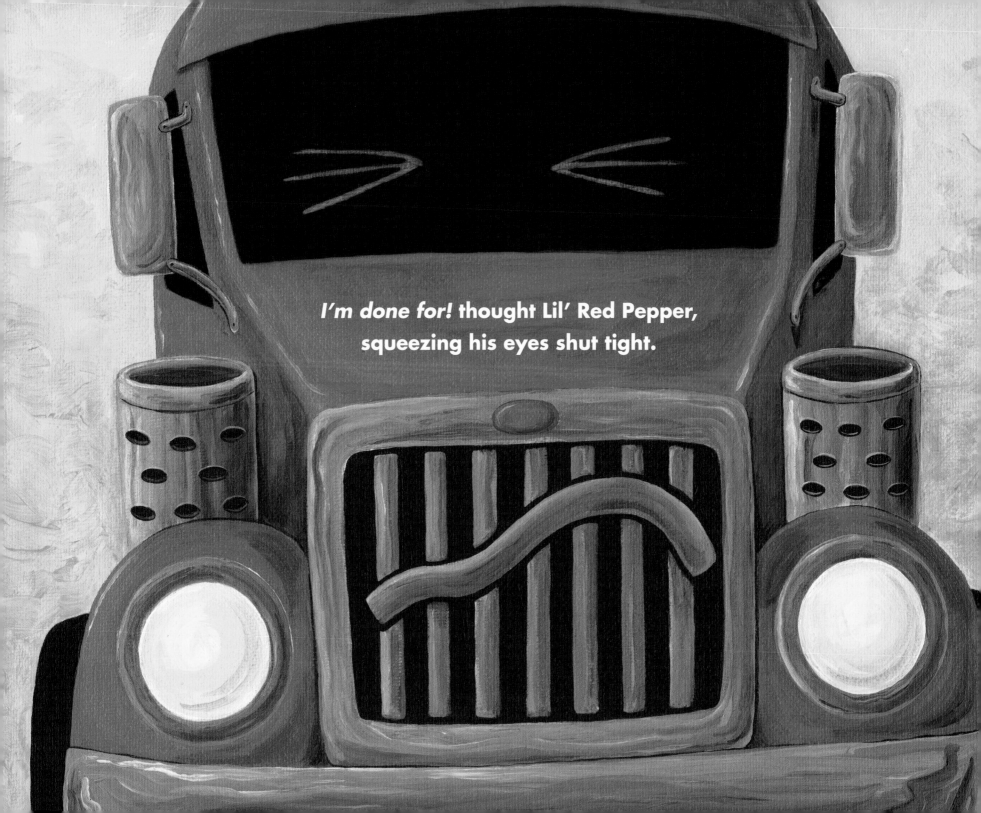

The ground was quaking, Lil' Red Pepper was shaking, and Tough Troy's deep voice rose over the rumbling, "Blue Barry, you can't go a week without smashing into something. Who are you to poke fun at another truck? Jersey Jay, just last month you crashed and tipped over trying to race Sassy Sal to the jobsite, and Sassy Sal, on your first day hauling gravel out of the quarry you drove off the haul road and got stuck same as Lil' Red Pepper."

Tough Troy didn't let up. "You don't know anything about him! He could be the greatest truck to ever haul out of the quarry, but you're poking fun and blowing smoke at him when he's stuck. Everybody makes mistakes." The whole quarry fell silent.

After a long while, Lil' Red Pepper opened his eyes and looked up from
the waning clouds of dust and smoke.
Tough Troy was gone.

But Lil' Red Pepper
was back on the haul road,
parked in the very front of the line.
All of that rumbling and shaking was Tough Troy pulling me out of
the sand and I didn't even realize it! I still have a chance
to haul today—PEPPER POWER!

Right then,
Leonard the Loader
showed up with a
bucket of gravel.
"Hey there,
Lil' Red Pepper,
let's get to work.
No time for
shilly-shally in
Cherry Grove."

What a great day! thought Lil' Red Pepper as he happily left the quarry to make his first delivery.

C'YA ON THE ROAD!